Peaches and Plum
in Trouble

ILLUSTRATED BY STEPHANIE BOEY
WRITTEN BY CAROLINE REPCHUK

SIENA

It was a bright, sunny morning at Tumbledown Orchard. Grandma was busy stirring a large pot of jam over the fire, when the twins scrambled into the kitchen for breakfast. "What's for breakfast, Grandma?" asked Peaches.

"Why, your favourite of course," said Grandma. "Toast and jam."

"Plum jam for me, please," said Plum.

"As if I would dare to give you anything else!" chuckled Grandma.

Just then Pa Jam ambled into the kitchen.

"Still eating breakfast?" he grumbled. "You should be up and about like the rest of us. I've been working in the garden since six o'clock this morning."

"So have we," whispered Peaches to Plum, with a giggle. Little did Pa know, but the naughty twins had been out in the garden early too. They had decided to play a trick on him.

Peaches and Plum were two of the cheekiest little pandas you could imagine. They were always up to mischief. Early that morning they had taken Pa's prize pears from the garden shed and hidden them. They knew that he would think Big Bamboo had eaten them. Pa had been planning to enter the pears in the Fruitgrower's Annual Show and he was very proud of them.

11

After breakfast, Peaches and Plum crept into the garden, hid behind a big raspberry bush and waited to see what would happen.

Their elder brother, Big Bamboo, was pretending to be hard at work as usual. But whenever Pa went off to fetch something, he would sneak into the blackcurrant patch for a crafty jam sandwich. He always kept a supply of them in his pocket, just in case of emergencies.

He had just finished tucking into a large blackcurrant jam sandwich and was having a quiet snooze, when all of a sudden he woke with a start. Pa was thundering down the garden towards him, shouting his name very loudly indeed! Big Bamboo shot to his feet.

14

Big Bamboo didn't know why Pa
looked so cross, but he wasn't going to stay
around to find out! He started to run as
fast as he could through the orchard.
"You've gone too far this time, you greedy
panda," called Pa running behind him.
"You'll be sorry when I catch up with you!"
Big Bamboo ran faster...

And faster!

In fact he ran so fast, that when he reached the stream at the end of the orchard he couldn't stop running in time, and he fell in with a great big SPLASH! "Help!" he called. "Get me out!"

Just as Pa was about to say that it served
Big Bamboo right for eating his prize pears,
he heard a loud giggle from behind the
raspberry bush. "Who is that giggling?"
he asked. "Out you come!" Peaches and Plum
came out from behind the bush looking very
guilty and blushing pink. "Do you two terrors
know where my prize pears are?"
asked Pa sternly.

Although Peaches and Plum were naughty, they did not tell lies. "We hid your pears," said Peaches, owning up. "We're very sorry. We didn't think you'd be so cross."

"We didn't damage them," said Plum. "They are in some flowerpots in the potting shed." "Let's go and take a look," said Pa.

Pa and the twins started to head back through the orchard.

"Hey!" called Big Bamboo from the stream. "What about me!" They had forgotten all about helping him!

Soon Big Bamboo had been pulled shivering
from the chilly water. Pa apologised for
blaming him before finding out the truth
about the pears. He sent him to the kitchen
to dry off and have an extra large helping
of blackcurrant jam to make him feel better.

As for the twins, they were not allowed
any jam for a whole week!
And what of Pa's prize pears? They were
none the worse for their adventure, and won
first prize at the Fruitgrower's Annual Show!

• **T H E   E N D** •